CW01665024

Voiceless Voices

the climate change collection

by The Poet Tess

First published in England February 2020

And While The Wind

And while the wind screams through the window
And the dust of ages flies in the face of reason,
Palms drip oil onto troubled waters;
A whale festers in phenols,
A calf the size of Manhattan falls off its polar shelf,
Moaning at the separation as a heifer
Does from its dam. Damned if it does or it don't.

And while the waters rise
How many coral graves ghost beneath the sea?
                                        We've seen it all before
                                        We've seen it all before

The very air waves confusion and deceit.
Good buys trounce good-byes to our tilted sphere.
Did you bid farewell to that bat, the bird, the toad,
That succulent tree or Silversword,
To the rhino on the horns of his dilemma,
Or the tortoise, tapanouli, and the tiger?

What will you say?
What will you say
When the world sticks in your throat?

Keep Calm & Carry On

[there's something they ain't telling us]

The Earth's flat
And that's that!

Made in seven days,
The Bible says.

We're all fine
If I got mine.

Keep calm
Carry napalm.

Tide's out of reach?
Life's a beach!

Won't live forever
Whatever the weather.

2020 Vision

December's moon was modest
Behind a sliver of lace
A celestial Rubens bottom
Delicate fabric in place.
It dove behind a cloud bank
Not to be seen again
Before bedtime.

Tonight it's bolder
Flaunting a piercing light
No more Scaredy Kitty
Sitting there, purring
In no hurry
On its regal flight
Crossing skies sublime.

I fear the dark left in its wake
A kind of madness
Where to run? Nowhere to hide
Waking to the sadness of the day
That one time was its pride
The solar system out of sight
Except by telescope. Or hearsay.

When the air cannot support
My lunar vision
What will the moon do then?

The Blame Game

It isn't the fault of the sun
The moon is not to blame
The rains that fall will kill us all
Their acid burns our guilty squirms
We hang our heads in shame

We are abashed, my friends,
And hang our heads in shame.

The Children of Hope

1. Greta

Do not bully this pig-tailed girl
Do not call her names
She's calling out her future
Calm, with passion, pin-points shame
She only wants a better one-day

At first just one
And then they come
Her modest smile of welcome
Reaching out with hope
It's no mere teen-aged trope
There's more in store than just a fun day

To practice what you preach
To tell the truth and teach
The laggards of the world
To gag excess
And unafraid join hands

Listen to this girl
She speaks your tongue
You can understand
Get down on your knees
To hear her words
If you want to save your land

2. Kiunga Fights Bad Water

Sun to the rescue in Kenya
Reversing the messes you made
You gave three hundred thousand kids
The water that killed them

Dead. Killed them dead.

Folk from a mere map-dot dare stare
At the sun, decide to share it
Work its magic on the sea
Refining the water of hope
Of life. A life of hope.

Desalination for a nation
For the children of hope.

3. Fionn's Attracted

This teen was attracted to Cork
Magnetically drawn,
He wanted to put a cork
In the river to clean it

Fionn hails from Ballydehob,
Where west Cork's been tainted by rain
He fights on the front against pollution
An eco-warrior, clad in imagination

The enemy declares itself:
Microplastics
But Fionn won't be fooled by multisyllables
He speaks plainly. Get that stuff out!

He donned his armour of magnets
Fashioned a blade, divided the waters
More effectively than Moses
He made them pure again

And took away the International Prize
At the Science Fair.

Voyager

His name evokes sagacity
Like propheteers of old
He cuddles our confusion
Explains the hot and cold
Of cloudy greenhouse Venus
And the spaces in between us
Icy cold and hot
From our little blue dot.

He waved the Voyager farewell
Unloosed its digital ties
The hold held crates of promise
Etched into a precious disk
And back to his desk
To confirm the calculation
That aliens could never meet
On our little blue dot.

Should, by some miracle of mind
And time and space,
The Voyager return
To speak the truth of galaxies
Far, far away
The profiteers will slay him
Just like truth-sayers before
Soothsayers of yore.

Here endeth the lesson today.

Doomsday

Down to the butt of the world
they trek, the Icefin team
of Brits and Yanks.
Questioning with frozen breath
a five year quest
to measure the metres of doom.
        Pine Island Bay
        Pine Island Bay
        The ice melts into Pine Island Bay

The ice is a glacier called Thwaite
or Doomsday and Ice Tongue
It's licking the butt of the world

Let's hope they're keeping warm
the Icefin team: snuggly duvets,
Mugs of hot cocoa
lest their funding descends
to the Amundsen bed
caught in the silt of the Sea
like so many trekkers of old
        Their PM "doesn't get it"
        And POTUS doesn't care.
You bet he will regret it,
when he turns his faucet of gold
or a plain old British tap...

and the Doomsday ice thuds out
bops 'em on the head
and kills 'em dead.

Ephemera

When you believe
You can walk on water
Remember
You do not leave
Any footprints

When you deny
Greenland's under melt ice
Remember
To bat your eye
against climate change

Global warming's just a myth-take
Rising tide, shmising-ti...

[Glug, glug, glug…]

rocks through snow

Black rocks peek over the snow
That should rest below

The air seethes
Rocks struggle to breathe

We've meddled
We've muddled
We've muddied the waters

Stones suffocate unto insanity
Who can recognise that puddle of humanity
We once called ourselves?

Obstacles in the Way

2020 vision - Australia
blinded by smoke
it's on fire

2020 vision - Palm Springs
blinded by water
it's over your head

2020 vision - Kilauea
blinded by lava
it's spewing the core

2020 vision - your eyes
blinded by parasitic worms
disoriented genes

Can you see clearly now?
Really?

Giving Up

Mary had a little lamb
Followed by a slice of ham
She has no beef with the meat she eats
It's up to her, it's down to her
Don't tell her what to do

Little Jack Horner
Sat in his corner
Eating a Christmas pie
The plum he pulled out was shrivelled by drought
The cream had curdled in the ladle
And he was sent to bed
Without any supper or a kind word

Jack and Jill went up the hill
To fetch a pail of water
The well was dry and full of rats
They jumped the pump and scared the tots
Who tumbled down and split their heads
On the rocky road to hell

The rich kids play on Paradise Way
With toys of gold and diamonds
Their silky Saluki puppies
Lick their faces as they die
From the vicious microbes in their bottled water
Just 60,000 bucks for nearly a litre of
Acqua di Cristallo Tributo a Modigliani

You want me to take this stuff seriously?
Seriously?

Summit

They greet
They sit
They meet
They are polite
And try to justify attendance
Flown in, not by balloon or angel's wings

Assuming they're entitled
To the planes of pollution
That they're more important
Than you

They stand
Offer hands
Ever polite
As they make for the runway
Running away
From a ticking time bomb
Ticking off the meeting from the list

The headlines just report the facts:
They've met.

But nothing gets done
Again

Questions for Capitalists

What's in there where your heart should be?
Is it stone? Is it ice?
A slice of bone?

What fills that space where your eyes should be?
Is it glass? Is it gel?
Or plastic from hell?

You look like me
And talk like me
You're grave and silly
You walk like me

So why can't you feel
Why can't you see

You're killing me
You're killing me

Pattern Recognition

Stating The Obvious

A high wall of laurels
bounds my view to the North.
It hides the house beyond,
masking the modesty of neighbours.

The Searching

Divisions come and fade.
Baffled by the patterns that we made,
the evolutionary legacy of ages,
our brains select, replacing the rage,

crushing to sand the chaos of rocks.
But 'spite our lens we cannot tell
which of thirty billion brain cells
transform us into Sherlocks.

Detecting ad hoc designs,
crafted by hand or lying about,
eyes, nose, maw... squinting for signs.
Then the wind roars. Look! they're out!

Cortical neurons jump for joy:
the momentary lady, the head of a boy.
Swimming in the sea foam, roasted in the meat,
another shaping cumulus above the waving wheat.

But time trots on, and here's a thing,
beneath the moon the wind has gone.
The laurel leaves reach out for Spring,
one giant head of shades revealed at dawn.

Just one, enormous, stares me down,
relentless. Its full-face conveys
no danger under a laurel crown.
I do not fear its patterned ways.

But the fickle wind returns,
calmed, romancing every leaf anew.
Against the high wall it relearns
its tricks to block my northern view.

The Recognition

Aurora's patterned lights, gifted from the sun,
brightening the ice, making unseen colours run.
Arcing the frozen circle, its melting music plays.
Who's left to test the compass? Now I am afraid.

what will we be drinking

what will we be drinking
when the poles have shed their ice
when the taps are clogged with plastic
and the pipes are full of lice

will we remember water
when our minds have turned to mush
when our protests have been silenced
and the excrement won't flush

what will they be drinking
in the palaces of power
will they toast with fizz and voddie
when bells toll the final hour

Elemental

We're all made of star stuff,
We're all made of dreams.

Our home is roots and rhisomes,
Silica and streams.

And if the sea is boiling hot,
And whether pigs have wings,

When suns collide, we cannot hide
Beneath the heavy things.

We're all in our element;
The gas clouds will not fail

To rebirth flea and elephant,
But the air is getting stale.

Your DNA gets in the way
For dips in oily pools.

Your riches can't begin to pay
The witching hour of fools.

No matter how much gold you trade
How generous your terms

Our planet's not a game well-played
Your brain conspires with worms.

aphorisms for the new age

carpe diem: carp's had its day; another extinction

the frozen north: the glacier's reached the attic

an apple a day: your blood has overshot your pesticide level

all that glistens isn't gold: the Sahara's on fire!

all for one and one for all: you're on your own

you can lead a horse to water, but you can't make it drink: what's a horse?

there are more fish in the sea: there's more plastic in the fish.

the grass is always greener: why are they painting the grass?

for all the good they do

It's time to praise those people
For all the good they do
To help a troubled planet
With a dedicated crew

A couple in Liberia
Enchanted by the chimps
Making chumps of riflemen
Who confiscate the infants
And sell their moms for mince.
Let's celebrate their ups and down
For all the good they do.

A man and wife in India
Appalled by barren land
It was getting out of hand
So they bought what once was jungle
Rewilding brought the rains
For the decade of their pains
The streams now teem, their dreams came true
For all the good they do

Who'd be a Panthera-phobe
In the foothills of Nepal
The tallest mountains on the globe
Where big cats failed to call
Across the jungle walls?
If they cannot find each other
They will die in isolation
They need a link cross nations
So a dying man crept through
Joining up the vegetation
Saving tigers on their way
For all the good they do

In Africa and Asia
Some pachyderms roam free
Their chains clipped off, they claim the paths
Scraping against the trees
Wallowing in mud baths
The legacy of Daphne, Katherine Connolly, and Lek
These women and their crews
Assure zoos must take a rain-check
Twining trunks confirm their gratitude
For all the good they do.

We learn of many rescuers
Who offer consolation
Care and rehabilitation
Wiping trauma from the babes
Bringing hope to senior beasts
Abused, confused, just waiting for a word
To ease the pain of desolation

On every continent they're dying
Can't you hear them crying
Donkeys, vultures, and Saola
Baby rhinos, baby apes
They're locked up for experiments
Their habitats are raped
For palm oil fields whose yields
Bring billions to the traders

And they try to buy the saviours
The dedicated saviours
They bad-mouth sanctuaries
Try to bribe the functionaries
Complicit through and through
Calling into question
All the good they do.

The Language of Leaves

If you live in the Borneo forest
You need signals to show you the way
It's cosy at night in your camp site
But you must go greet the day
You must venture into the jungle
With your blow-pipe to hunt wild pig
And you need to say hi to your neighbours
When a storm is due and the harvest is big

The Borneo tribes have a system
They never studied at school
It's passed down the generations
So everyone knows the rules
It's fool-proof!

The language of leaves
Signals left in the trees
A language of sharing and care
Courtesy and kindness all in the open air

They call the system oroo
Anthropologists in the west
They agree it's very ingenious
And passes every test
Of effective communication
Who would have guessed
That a stick and a leaf
Folded into a sheath
Stuck into the ground
Could speak without sound
To anyone around who can read it

Come quickly. Bring water.
No don't go that way.
I'm in a good mood.
We've slaughtered a lizard
There's plenty of food
So please come and join us.
We'll share it with you.
Let's have a party.

We need a new plan
There are strangers around
A very bad man
Wants to cut down our woods
Our food plants and cures
We're waiting for you
What's ours is now yours.

If we work together
They will not take our land
We will share our future
They cannot understand
Our language of leaves

We are written in the leaves
Can you read us?
Better heed us!

You Cannot Conceive What You've Never Encountered

ET and fellow scholars at their charts
had gathered round to celebrate
the success [at last!] of the coalescence
of fuel-less fuel and route-less route
and to calculate possibilities:
which of their nearest galaxies they might visit
in the spirit of friendship
you understand, no notion of invasion
or domination even entering their mind-less minds.

They plotted the cost-benefit of heading this way
and that. Not all sweetness and light, by any means.
There were laugh-less laughs, a few barb-less barbs.
But no fights or altercations, and I'll swear to that,
even if I knew to whom I might swear.

One scholar wanted to consider a spiral arm,
quite insignificant, tucked away in the outer reaches
of... and here the scholar pronounced an identifying tag
in a language they all understood. But I don't,
and nor do you. So let's just say
they meant The Milky Way.

They didn't hold them all to scrutiny,
all those destinations. Their instruments
of measurement and more subtle data
signalled something was the matter, something
at the core. The centre of some galaxies
pulled with force-less force, pulled them
down into a black hole with gentle grace.
Inevitable. And something whispered "Alice."

It was certainly worth consideration, that blue-less blue
ball of gas, that star encircled by enticing worlds.
But one by one the pros were stifled by the cons
against the prospect of respect, of mutuality.
And for a time-less time, a solid ball of water-less water
waved the arms of its desperate denizens. Were they
seeking help or destruction?

So ET and chums turned their gaze elsewhere,
to forge concords of goodwill.
And the Earthlings [you and I],
who might have heard the music of the spheres,
would never conceive what we'd never encountered.

Jokers

Must be a joke, surely.
Nope, he tweeted it.
He tweets all his stuff overnight.
He tweets, so it must be so.

So, what, you saying it's no joke?
Of course, it's no joke.
This is serious stuff.
Yeah, so what did he say again?

He sez there's no such thing.
No such thing as climate change?
That's what he sez.
He's in charge, so he must know.

Must be a joke, surely.
What's that noise?
Oh, yeah, he awarded the contract.
The drilling contract.

Drilling? Where? For what? For why?
Up in the Bering Sea. Down, down, down.
Drilling down for gas. For oil. For jobs.
No such thing as climate change.

Making money ain't no joke.
Do we know a hoax when we see it?
Well, do we, folks?

Hydration

You cannot drink a glass of gas
Ice is nice to cool your booze
But don't be bamboozled
When it drifts in sheets past your window upstairs;
You get more than a fright, confused and bemused.

You can total the numbers in columns
Study stacks upon stacks of the stats
Yes, they will astound you
Be you round as a wombat or diplomat

You just can't get by without water.
You know it's the liquid of life
I'll bet you a quid
Be you acorn or squid...

By golly, by gosh and by heck...

You will turn up your toes
If you turn off the hose.
So what is this crap
Coming out of my tap?

Now, to whom shall I make out the cheque?

The Strand

I hear you little seal pup
You are crying like a babe
I wish that I could help
I can tell that you are dying
From entanglements
That mangle your poor neck
And the wounds around your flippers
As you wash up on the sand

But my legs no longer hold me
I wobble when I stand
And the hurdy gurdy plays
Its tunes down on the sand
I hear its jolly music on the strand

My poor forlorn leviathan
I hear your screams of anguish
I wish that I could help
You are crying underwater as you die
From the painful ceaseless slaughter
Of the military missions
Signalling positions, louder
Than your sonar
Just explosions and confusion
Whale songs bleed to wailing
Assailing your cetacean ears

But they fill me up with fear
That military band
And the hurdy gurdy plays
Its tunes down on the sand
I hear its jolly tunes along the strand

Time & Tide

We're running out of time
Running out of road
The tide foams in, the tide retreats
The ocean cannot hold

Tickety-tickety tock
The mice have wound the clock
They've scoffed their meal and cannot feel
The gentle gas that slays 'em

Instead of farming wind
Investing billions for a bunker
Besuited blokes tell sexist jokes
And taxes soar to pays 'em

No matter what they do
It ain't all tickety-boo.

Time and the tide wait for no mouse
Nor human bean or tiny louse
Hold! Hold back the water!
Stick a cork in a bottle
That'll stopple its escape

The tide surrounds our island home
Offshore the waves can
Lullaby our power, or tower
With the rage of rotting potatoes
The sea could fuel our daily lives
No matter when the wind blows

If wonky bankers dipped their tootsies
In the drink, they'd know they oughta
Take it littorally, to the brink
And strictly rule the waves
Instead of waiving them for gain.

More jobs are no excuse for
The ruin of the world.
We're running out of time,
The tide is waiting.

Are you watching on the dock
Staring at the clock?
Tickety-tickety-tickety tock.

Bumble

Bridle and van Rensburg:
they're Bristol based and know their bees.
The buzzers are failing,
failing to buzz. It's down to uz.

Bridle and van Rensburg
know their bees, and here's what they sez:
Alarming. The evidence is alarming.
It's ringing alarm bells.

Bridle and van Rensburg:
from Bristol comes the word.
They're investigating bees,
Bumbles, buzzers, shy Loners.

Bridle and van Rensburg
know all the bumblebees.
Yellow-throated, carder, all the rest.
two-hundred-and-fifty messengers of sadness.

Bridle and van Rensburg know
those pollinators fail to fly; they're dying.
Without them you and I and all the life beneath the sky
will also die, bumbling towards destruction.

Bridle and van Rensburg
can link the bees to a dwindle,
a climate emergency, they sound the alarm
Bio-diversity's down on the farm.

The farmers keep spraying
The soil keeps decaying
The bumbles keep dying
The world keeps denying.

Stranded

all at sea

Locked on a ship
As big as a mountain
Locked in on a ship
Becalmed atop the waves

But no one's calm, or waves
To the inmates locked inside with no mates
Cut off, not cut out for going out
No window on the world

Fed with special foodstuffs
Served by stiff-armed robots
Armed to the teeth with dental records
For identification purposes
Providing water pure as angel sighs
Pure as unicorn pee
[The way they neigh and run away]

we cannot see the danger

With a rum-tum-tum the carers come
Boots as steady as a drum-roll
clad in haz-chem suits
From follicles atop the head
Toeing down the distal phalanx
Every millimetre protected
in a portable piece of safety
where even your clothing breathes for you.
The cloth, the cloth is breathing.
In two three and out two three
In two three and out two three

Impossible to hold a secret
Whispers slide between the air-tight joints

it's the not knowing...

News floats down the levels
Of the ship
News of life and death
Of sickness, yucky snot
And tortured deaths
Contorted joints
Exploding lungs
Rumours or facts?
Packed up, tactless.
The whispers come
Down the levels
To the beat of their drum.

a truth to be told

When the end is close
When viscous strands of spit
Hang from the gum line
When the plumb line means
The unicorn has kicked the bucket
And the stranded ship
Goes down a storm
None can hold out futile arms
To block the suits from suicide
And jumping in the beckoning waves

Remember the world watched flickers
Images on tee-vee
Of couples holding fast
Through the vastness of the air
As they cascaded to the ground
Ground zero, ground into dust
When the towers were no longer there?

Some people on the stranded ship…
The ship as big as a mountain
The ship becalmed at sea…
Ask if they're infected or protected?
The world waits for an answer
The world is desperate to know
In every cabin, on each deck
There lurks a threat. It owes a debt
To Schrödinger and his questions
Of quantum. Little solace.

just gotta get on with it

The death toll is rising
Yet also slowing down.
[Not slower than no deaths]
But in every cabin, on each deck
Of their maritime jail
The quality of life
Is being contained
No mercy
They're restrained,
Comfy as can be
In the circumstances,
Stranded and all at sea.

Perhaps they're protected
But they're also rejected

Infected or protected?
And no port will take them
The world will forsake them
Though they've past the Quantum Tests.
Their blood's been probed and sampled,
Its cells flow virus free.
Yet no port will accept them.

you ain't seen nothing yet

What do you know of Svarlbard
And of the Siberian woods?
Or Bethel in Alaska?
Maybe, my friends, you should.

For the Schrödinger test aboard that ship
Will dive and dip and slip in the ice
Somewhat containable, even sustainable.

There's really no comparison
With the monsters released in the North
When Bethel turns to goo, there is no place to go.
We watched the highway buckle
I know you saw it too.

Tinier than the fabled Riders
Yet more apocalyptic
Allow me to present
Lady Ann Thrax, wotta gal!
The bopper they call Smalls, a Pox indeed.
Mister Colin Era, Col for short, the H is silent!
And Granny Pox, the Bubbie, known as Buboe or the plague.

Better check your temperature
Are you brooding swollen glands
Can your heart compete at Ascot
Can you move your frozen hands?

Thought you were safe from monsters
Imprisoned underground?
The Perma-Frost is melting.
Its centre can't be found.
Best think again, my friend.
Time to think again.

crimes against nature

Consider a small Siberian boy
Burning with ague
No blanket stops his shivers
When Ann Thrax & Co. escape with the melt
Microbes allied to strangle his heart
A ferocious anaconda.
He couldn't last past sundown
Organs rotting in the heat.
He was so small
But anthrax smaller still
More powerful
Has all it needs to kill

When Frost is not so Perma
Core temperatures keep rising
Melting the hard, hard ground
Not surprising
Beneath Siberian wood

Not far away in Norway
There's a bank where wild times grow;
A store beneath the snow
A stash of plants to feed us
When the forest does not need us
When the world has gone to seed
Saving soya, plums, and rice.

But Frost is not so Perma
Core temperatures keep rising
Melting the hard, hard ground
Unsurprising
Beneath the Svalbard ice.

When will we take our last breath
Unprotected from virulent death?
I suspect we're already infected
Don't you?

Dead By Then

Squabblers place their bets
Gambling on the future, but
I'll be dead by then

Doom lurks out of sight
Whispering false promises
You'll be dead by then

Someday the guiltless
Sun will show us proper warmth
We'll all be dead by then

Dear Diary 2099

All the leaves are brown
and the skies are grey.
Since I was a tiny tot
They've always been that way.

I'm dreaming of a time
I can go outside to play;
but Robo-Doc will not allow it,
waves my pleas away.

For the air is poison
Poison, poison
The air is poison
And we're locked inside our rooms

The seas are poison
Poison, poison
The seas are poison
We are doomed.

They said they would take care of us
I found a book that claimed it
Now all the books have turned to dust
No one is left to name it.

The land is poison
Poison, poison
The land is poison
Why, oh why, oh why...
Why have you left us to die?

Printed in Poland
by Amazon Fulfillment
Poland Sp. z o.o., Wrocław

54493894R00026